The Darling Boys

BRADBURY PRESS • NEW YORK

Maxwell Macmillan Canada • Toronto
Maxwell Macmillan International
New York • Oxford • Singapore • Sydney

The Darling Boys

By M. C. HELLDORFER

Illustrated by MEGAN HALSEY

Bradbury Press
Macmillan Publishing Company
866 Third Avenue
New York, NY 10022

Maxwell Macmillan Canada, Inc.
1200 Eglinton Avenue East
Suite 200
Don Mills, Ontario M3C 3N1

Macmillan Publishing Company is part of the Maxwell Communication
Group of Companies.

First American edition
Printed and bound in Hong Kong by South China Printing Company
(1988) Ltd.
10   9   8   7   6   5   4   3   2   1

The illustrations were done in pen and ink and watercolor. They were color-separated
by scanner and reproduced in four colors using red, blue, yellow, and black inks.
The text of this book is set in 15 point Caslon 224.
Typography by Julie Quan

LIBRARY OF CONGRESS CATALOGING-IN-PUBLICATION DATA
Helldorfer, Mary Claire, date
The darling boys / by M.C. Helldorfer ; illustrated by Megan
Halsey.—1st American ed.
p.   cm.
Summary: A baker's daughter devises a clever scheme to outwit her
thieving brothers and recover the gold they've been stealing from
her and her mother.
ISBN 0-02-743516-4
[1. Brothers and sisters—Fiction.   2. Bakers and bakeries—
Fiction.]   I. Halsey, Megan, ill.   II. Title.
PZ7.H37418Dar   1992
[E]—dc20   91-44708

A NOTE FROM THE AUTHOR
The inspiration for this book was the medieval ballad, "Get up and Bar the Door," first
published in eighteenth-century collections of Scottish songs. Interested readers can
hunt down analogues of this adult tale in cultures as diverse as French, Italian, Arabic,
and Turkish. (See F. J. Child's *The English and Scottish Popular Ballads*.)

For my sister Anne,
riding toward her dream
—MCH

To Steve and Marty,
my favorite boys
—MH

Some say the baker of Hornchurch rests in peace, glad to be rid of his foolish wife and quarreling sons. But surely he misses his daughter, Vi, who baked with him half the night and carried bread to market twice a day. Perhaps the old baker lies in his grave, smiling now at the cleverness of his youngest child.

The day began like any other. "Well, my darling boys," the baker's widow said to her sons, Swindle and Gyp, "Vi and I are off to market. Sing and bake as you love to do, my darling boys, and don't forget to lock the door. Robbers are everywhere.

"Heaven forbid anything should happen to my darling boys."

Now, these boys hated to work, and each had a secret plan to run away. So each stole from the family pot: one piece of the gold Vi and her mother brought home each day.

Swindle hid his gold in a rusted water kettle that hung by the hearth. Gyp saved his money in jars of peach jam. These were, in fact, their favorite hiding places since they were small boys.

On this day that started like every other, Gyp eyed his jars of jam, and Swindle patted his kettle. Then they baked a little and sang a lot. It was something like opera:

"Brother Swindle, dear brother Swindle, please mix the flour and salt."

"Brother Gyp, dear brother Gyp, please roll out the dough, brother Gyp."

But then the song got a little off-key.

"Brother Swindle, knead the dough. Knead the dough, Swindle. Now!"

"Gyp, dough-brain Gyp. It's your turn. Shape it."

Soon the boys were shouting at each other.

"Knead it, Swindle."

"Braid it, Gyp."

"Butter it, Swindle!"

"Bake it, Gyp!"

They shouted louder and louder—

"Mix it!"

"Roll it!"

"Knead it!"

"Shape it!"

—faster and faster—

"Knead it!"

"Braid it!"

"Butter it!"

"Bake it!"

Pieces of dough flew back and forth across the room. Sometimes the brothers caught the dough. Sometimes the dough hit the ceiling and stuck to the walls. Now and then it sailed through the open door.

So much hung from the rafters and walls that, when Vi returned at noon, they had baked but one loaf of bread to sell at market. The girl scraped what dough she could into pans. Then she quieted her brothers, and warned them twice to close and lock the door.

But Vi wasn't ten feet down the road when she heard her brothers arguing through the open door:

"Mix it!"

"Roll it!"

  "Lock the door!"

"Knead it!"

"Shape it!"

  "Lock the door!"

"Knead it!"

"Braid it!"

  "Lock the door!"

"Butter it!"

"Bake it!"

  "Lock the door!"

Vi shook her head; then she turned down a road other than the one to market.

Now the two boys did mix, roll, knead, shape, knead, braid, butter, and bake—a little. But neither one would get up to lock the door. At last, his throat sore from screaming, Swindle said to his brother, "Whoever speaks first has to lock the door."

Well, the room grew very quiet. The boys worked more quickly than they ever had and were nearly done when a shadow darkened the bakery entrance. There stood a stranger, wrapped in a scarf and long coat, shaded by a hat. Dark gloves clutched an empty bag.

"Pardon me," the stranger said in a hushed voice. "Could you tell me the way to market? I am very hungry and would like some bread and tea."

Now, Swindle knew the market was closing. He was just about to say so, when he saw his brother smiling. Remembering their pact, he quickly shut his mouth.

"Eh?" said the stranger.

But neither brother spoke.

"I said I am hungry. Perhaps you would be kind enough to sell me a piece of bread and a cup of tea."

At that Gyp jumped up, ready to charge the stranger for three loaves of bread and four kettles of tea. Then he saw his brother smiling. Remembering their pact, he quickly shut his mouth.

"Eh?" said the person with the empty bag.

But neither brother spoke.

"Well then, I will have to help myself," the stranger said, reaching for the rusted kettle that hung next to the hearth. "Great butter buns!" the stranger exclaimed. "This kettle is heavy as gold!"

Now Swindle leaped forward and was about to speak. Then he saw his brother smiling and quickly shut his mouth.

The stranger set the water to boil.

What a rattling there was! The old teakettle shook, shook, shook, and through its spout blew a shower of yellow coins.

"Delicious," remarked the stranger, filling the empty bag with boiled gold. "Perhaps I'll try your bread and jam."

Now Gyp rushed forward and was about to speak. Then he saw his brother smiling. Quickly he shut his mouth.

The stranger spread a piece of bread thick with peach jam and bit down. *Chnk.*

The stranger bit again and spat—*chnk clank*—then chewed on through three jars of peach jam—*chnk clank, chnk clank, chnk clank.*

Gathering up the gold, the stranger hurried out the door. Just then the widow came down the road from market. She saw the mysterious figure leap onto a horse. "Stop, thief!" she shouted.

The stranger whirled the horse about and, leaning down to the widow, dropped gold into her hands. "I give you back half, madam. Guard it well from those two."

Then horse and rider rushed off toward the moon.

The old woman ran inside, much bewildered. Had she been robbed, or given a gift? She called out, "My darling boys, what happened? Did you forget to lock the door?"

"I told you to do it, Gyp!" Swindle said.

Then Gyp laughed and stamped his foot. "You spoke first. Now *you* get up and lock the door!"

So the darling boys lived at the bakery, arguing ever after.

As for Vi, she has a fine shop in the next town, which she
bought with her warm and sticky gold.